Don't count the number of birthdays. Count how happy you feel. I'm Birthday Bear, and I'll help make your birthdays the best ever.

I'm Wish Bear, and if you wish on my star, maybe your special dream will come true.

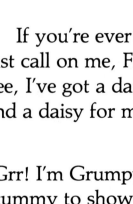

If you're ever feeling lonely, just call on me, Friend Bear. See, I've got a daisy for you and a daisy for me.

Grr! I'm Grumpy Bear. There's a cloud on my tummy to show that I take the grouchies away, so you can be happy again.

I'm Love-a-Lot Bear. I have two hearts on my tummy. One is for you; the other is for someone you love.

It's my job to bring you sweet dreams. I'm Bedtime Bear, and right now I'm a bit sleepy. Are you sleepy, too?

Now that you know all of us, we hope that you'll have a special place for us in your heart, just like we do for you.

With love from all of us,

The Care Bears

Copyright © 1984 by American Greetings Corp. All rights reserved.
Published in the United States by Parker Brothers, Division of CPG Products Corp.

Care Bears, Care Bears Logo, Tenderheart Bear, Friend Bear, Grumpy Bear, Birthday Bear, Cheer Bear, Bedtime Bear, Funshine Bear, Love-a-Lot Bear, Wish Bear and Good Luck Bear are trademarks of American Greetings Corporation, Parker Brothers, authorized user.

Library of Congress Cataloging in Publication Data: Winthrop, Elizabeth. Being brave is best. A Tale from the Care Bears.
SUMMARY: Afraid to go to the hospital to have her tonsils out, Jenny is helped get over her fear by Cheer Bear and his friend.
[1. Tonsillectomy—Fiction. 2. Hospitals—Fiction. 3. Sick—Fiction. 4. Bears—Fiction] I. Title. II. Series.
PZ7.W768Be 1984 [E] 83-23696 ISBN 0-910313-19-9
Manufactured in the United States of America 1 2 3 4 5 6 7 8 9 0

A Tale from the Care Bears

Being Brave is Best

Story by Elizabeth Winthrop
Pictures by Tom Cooke

On Monday Jenny was playing with her friends, Annie and Beth. They were turning the rope and Jenny was jumping. Beth chanted:

"All, all, all in together, girls;
How do you like the weather, girls?
January, February . . . Jenny, why did you stop?"

"My throat hurts," Jenny said.

"Not again," Annie said. "Your throat is always hurting."

"Dr. Williams told my mother if I got one more sore throat, they'd have to do something about it," Jenny said. "I'm not going to tell my mother about this one."

On Tuesday Jenny felt worse. Her throat hurt so much, she couldn't drink her orange juice at breakfast.

"Jenny, you don't look very well," her father
said. "Are you sure you feel all right?"

Jenny jumped up from the table. "I feel great.
I'd better go, or I'll be late for school."

In math class Mrs. Burnett asked Jenny to do a problem at the board. When Jenny went to the board she felt dizzy, and she got the whole problem wrong.

"Jenny, you look very pale," Mrs. Burnett said. She felt Jenny's forehead. "Why, you are burning up. You go right down and see the nurse."

The nurse took Jenny's temperature. When she read the thermometer, she called Jenny's mother at once. Her mother picked Jenny up and took her directly to Dr. Williams's office. The doctor put a wooden stick on Jenny's tongue and made her say "aahh." She looked in Jenny's ears and up her nose.

"Jenny, you get dressed while I talk to your mother in the next room," Dr. Williams said.

Jenny began to feel frightened. Why couldn't the doctor speak in front of her? Did Dr. Williams know that she had something terrible? What was going to happen to her?

While Jenny was getting dressed, she thought that she heard something about tonsils and hospitals. "Oh help," Jenny thought.

Soon Dr. Williams came back into the room.
She sat down right next to Jenny.

"Jenny, I'm going to give you some pills to
help you feel better now, but next week you are
going to the hospital so that I can take those
tonsils out. You don't need them any more. They
are very large and sore, and they make your throat
hurt."

"Will it hurt?" asked Jenny.

"You will be asleep during the operation," Dr. Williams answered, "so you won't feel a thing. But when you wake up after the operation, your throat will hurt a little bit. Don't worry. It won't take long for you to feel just fine again. After this, Jenny, you won't have those nasty sore throats anymore." Dr. Williams stood up. "Now I want you to go home and think about what I said. If you have questions, you can call me anytime."

Jenny and her mother slowly drove home.

"Dr. Williams says your daddy and I can spend the night in the hospital with you, so we can be near you the whole time," her mother said.

Jenny didn't answer. She was trying to be brave. She wasn't going to talk about the hospital. She wasn't even going to think about it. She would think about something nice instead, she decided; something like horseback riding.

But that night Jenny couldn't get to sleep. Her throat hurt and it was hard to think about anything else. She wondered what it would be like to spend the night in a great big hospital. She curled up tight and put her head under her pillow. Suddenly she heard a pleasant voice calling her name.

"Hello, Jenny. Come on out from under that pillow! Why, I slid all the way down a rainbow from the land of Care-a-lot just to see you."

Jenny peeked out. There, sitting on her bed was a pink Bear with a rainbow on her tummy.

"Hello. I'm Cheer Bear. My friends, the other Care Bears, and I are always watching out for people who are sad or scared." The fuzzy pink Bear cuddled up next to Jenny. "Now tell me what's bothering you."

"I am trying to be brave. I don't want to talk about it." Jenny sniffed. She was about to cry.

Cheer Bear, who always knew just the right thing to say, answered, "Being brave and being quiet are two different things. How can people help you if you won't tell them what's wrong?" Then the little pink Bear skipped across the room and turned on the light. "That's better," Cheer Bear said. "Now we can see what we are saying! Ha-ha."

So Jenny told Cheer Bear about her sore throat and the hospital and the operation.

"Doesn't it feel a little better now that you've told someone?" asked Cheer Bear as she settled herself down on the bed.

"I guess so," Jenny answered.

"I know it's a little scary to think about going into the hospital. But remember," added Cheer Bear, who always knew just the right thing to say, "your mother and father will be there with you. Doctor Williams is a fine doctor, who knows everything about tonsils." Cheer Bear smiled. "And all of us in Care-a-lot are going to be looking down and thinking of you."

"Are you really?" Jenny asked.

"Sure we are." Cheer Bear gave Jenny a soft, cozy hug and tucked her sheets in again. "Now you'd better go back to sleep."

"Will you come back and see me again?" Jenny asked.

"I'll send my good friend, Funshine Bear. He'll come and see you in the hospital. Don't forget to look for him," Cheer Bear called as she turned off the light.

Jenny watched as Cheer Bear walked up a rainbow that suddenly appeared outside her window. She smiled and soon was fast asleep.

"Today's the day," Jenny's mother said one morning during the next week. "Dr. Williams is expecting you." She reached down and gave Jenny's hand a squeeze.

Jenny got up and packed her suitcase with her favorite pajamas, her toothbrush, and her soft, cuddly doll.

She ate her breakfast very slowly.

She said goodbye to her two goldfish.

Then she got into the car with her mother and
father.

When they got to the hospital, her mother had to fill out some papers at the front desk, so Jenny's father took her up to her room. They walked down a long hall. Nurses were bustling back and forth, carrying trays. Jenny heard someone crying.

"I'm a little bit scared, Daddy," said Jenny.

Jenny's father leaned down and scooped her up. It felt good to be carried even though Jenny knew that she was really too old for that sort of thing.

A nurse with a nice smile came up to them. "You must be Jenny," she said. "We've been waiting for you. My name is Miss Kent. I'll show you your room."

Jenny had a small sunny room with a bed by the window.

"There is a drawer here for your toothbrush and your hair ribbons," said Miss Kent. "Here is a closet where you can hang up your clothes."

Then she pointed to a button next to the pillow. "Anytime you need something, Jenny, you just push this button, and I'll come check on you. See you later."

Jenny's father helped her change into her pajamas.

"I'm just going to find Mommy," he said. "I'll be right back."

Jenny looked around the room. There were pretty paintings on the wall, but there was a funny looking machine on the wall right above her head. Jenny hugged her doll close. She didn't want to be in this hospital. She wanted to go home.

"Psst, Jenny, I'm down here," said a merry
voice. There, peeking up from the side of her bed,
was a yellow Bear.

"Oh, you must be Funshine Bear," Jenny cried. "Cheer Bear said that you'd come to visit me."

Funshine Bear did a little dance and jumped up onto Jenny's bed. "And here I am. How are you, Jenny? All of us up in the land of Care-a-lot have been thinking about you."

"I'm a little scared, Funshine. This hospital is so big. I want to be in my own room again."

"But look outside, Jenny. The sun is shining and the birds are singing. Look on the bright side of things. This afternoon the operation will be all over. In no time at all, you'll be back at school, playing with your friends, and enjoying ice cream."

"And no more sore throats," said Jenny.

"That's right," said Funshine with a little giggle. "Now you're looking on the bright side of things. Aha! I hear some important people coming, so I have to go. Remember, we're thinking about you up there." Then Funshine hopped off the bed, once again did a little dance, and vanished in the wink of an eye. Jenny looked under the bed. He wasn't there, and he wasn't in the closet either. She tiptoed to her door to see who was coming, and she almost bumped into Dr. Williams and her parents.

"Why, Jenny, you're just the person I was coming to see," said Dr. Williams. "How are you feeling?"

"I'm a little scared," Jenny said. "But I don't want any more sore throats, and I know tomorrow I'll feel glad you took these dumb tonsils out."

"That's what I like to hear," said Dr. Williams. "Hop up on this bed. We're ready to go."

The nurse came and gave Jenny a shot. It hurt a little bit, but soon Jenny began to feel sleepy. She held her mother's hand as Dr. Williams pushed the bed down the long hall.

Just before Jenny fell asleep she remembered Funshine's little dance. She smiled and closed her eyes.

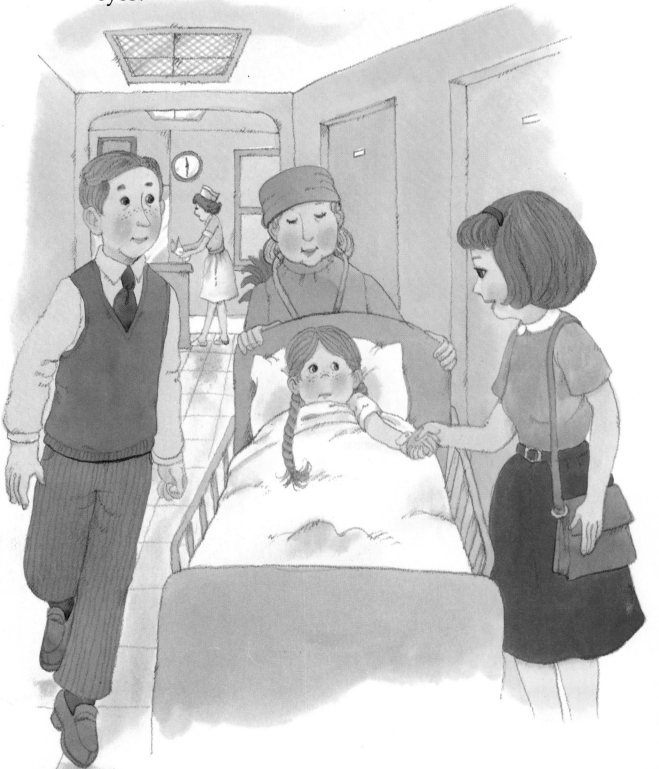

When Jenny woke up after the operation, her mother and father were sitting by the bed.

"Hello, Jenny," her father said. "How do you feel?"

"Sleepy," said Jenny. She looked out the window. "The sun is still shining, isn't it, Funshine Bear?" she whispered.

"What did you say dear?" her mother asked.

But Jenny didn't answer. She had already gone back to sleep.

The next week Jenny was back skipping rope with Beth and Annie.

"Got a sore throat today, Jenny?" Annie teased.

"Of course not," said Jenny. "And I'm glad I went to the hospital. It wasn't really bad at all." And then Jenny jumped over the rope and chanted:

"One, two, and nothing to fear.
I've got friends named Funshine and Cheer!"